orca
limelights

Off Pointe

Leanne Lieberman

ORCA BOOK PUBLISHERS

Library and Archives Canada Cataloguing in Publication

Lieberman, Leanne, 1974–, author
Off pointe / Leanne Lieberman.
(Orca limelights)

Issued in print and electronic formats.
ISBN 978-1-4598-0280-3 (pbk.).--ISBN 978-1-4598-0281-0 (pdf).--
ISBN 978-1-4598-0282-7 (epub)

I. Title. II. Series: Orca limelights
PS8623.I36O34 2014   jc813'.6   C2014-901555-0
C2014-901556-9

First published in the United States, 2014
Library of Congress Control Number: 2014935396

Summary: Meg lives for ballet and doesn't like to try new things, so a
summer at camp learning new dance styles proves challenging.

*Orca Book Publishers is dedicated to preserving the environment and has
printed this book on Forest Stewardship Council® certified paper.*

Orca Book Publishers gratefully acknowledges the support for
its publishing programs provided by the following agencies:
the Government of Canada through the Canada Book Fund and the
Canada Council for the Arts, and the Province of British Columbia
through the BC Arts Council and the Book Publishing Tax Credit.

Cover design by Rachel Page
Cover photography by Getty Images

ORCA BOOK PUBLISHERS   ORCA BOOK PUBLISHERS
PO Box 5626, STN. B   PO Box 468
Victoria, BC Canada   Custer, WA USA
v8R 6s4   98240-0468

www.orcabook.com
Printed and bound in Canada.

17 16 15 14 • 4 3 2 1

In memory of Debra Karby

One

As I wait in the wings to go onstage, my hands stroke the fine tulle of my pink tutu. The rest of the junior company is already under the bright lights, and in a moment I will step onto the stage for my solo. My muscles are warm, my hair secured in its bun, my pointe shoes laced tightly around my ankles. Shivers run up my arms as I watch the other dancers circle the stage in neat piqué turns in time to the music. At this moment all the aching muscles and late nights cramming homework are worth it. The music slows, and I count eight beats. Then I take a deep breath, compose my face and step en pointe to join the other dancers.

For two glorious minutes I dance in the center of the stage. I perform entrechat-quatre—jumping and rapidly beating my feet together—into pirouettes. My jumps are high, my turns steady, all my lines neat. A trickle of sweat runs down my back as I prepare for the final pirouette, my right leg kicking out to propel my turn, my arms coming to second position. I finish with an arabesque, one leg gracefully extended behind me, and then a curtsy. There's a pop of applause, and then I run offstage.

Back in the wings, my breath speeds up and a smile starts to spread across my face. My first solo. There's no time for celebration, nothing more than a nod from Mrs. G, who is concentrating on the other dancers still onstage, her hands supporting her lower back. There are only two more numbers before I join the rest of the company for the finale, the "Dance of the Cygnets" from *Swan Lake*. Quick, quick, down the stairs with the other dancers to the dressing room to change my pink tutu for a white one. There's just enough time to towel off, adjust my toe shoes and fix the smear of eyeliner at the corner of my eye. Then we're back in the wings, the music starting up, Mrs. G counting us in. And then we are onstage and I am dancing.

Minutes later, when the curtain falls to a roar of applause, I want the evening to start all over again.

Afterward, the dressing room is full of excited dancers, everyone hugging and congratulating each other. My best friend, Julia, throws her arms around me. "Worth it?" she says, but it's not really a question. We both know ballet is worth everything. A moment later we are overwhelmed with parents and friends all pressing us with flowers.

We are ballerinas, and tonight is our night.

* * *

I wake the next morning tired but happy and roll over in bed to check my phone. There are messages from Julia, from my other ballet friends and from my aunt Cathy. Then I notice an email from Mrs. G. I open the message, expecting it to be a note of congratulations, but it's entitled "With Regrets."

Mrs. G writes:

I regret to inform you that the Summer Ballet Program is canceled due to my unexpected back surgery. I will see you all in the fall.

Fondly,

Elaine Greer

I lie in bed, stunned. I always attend the summer ballet program. And this year I was even going to stay in the residence for the first time while my parents are away in Italy. Tears start to form in my eyes as I call Julia. She's read the email too and is also in tears. "What will you do?" she asks.

"I don't know," I tell her. I've never done anything but ballet.

My ballet obsession began when I was four and my parents took my sister Tess and me to see a performance of *The Nutcracker*. I remember the thrill that came over me when the curtain went up. I sat on the edge of my seat as the beautiful ballerinas turned and leaped across the stage. Tess liked when the soldiers fought the mice, but I loved when Clara danced with the prince. I begged my parents for ballet classes, for ballet costumes, ballet books and ballet music. I've been dancing ever since.

* * *

The next week creeps by. I've survived grade nine, and school is out. Everyone else has summer jobs lined up, but all I can think is, I'm supposed to be at ballet school. I try hanging out at the mall and walking in the park, things I think I want to do when I'm busy with ballet, but I have no one to hang out with. My ballet friends have scattered across the city, and Julia is working at her parents' restaurant. I don't have any school friends because I leave early and spend all my lunch hours working on the homework I don't have time to do at night.

Mom keeps asking me what I want to do while she and Dad go to Italy for two weeks, but all I can say is "Ballet." I know she thinks I'm being difficult, but when I close my eyes I only see myself at the barre.

* * *

"Meg, special breakfast for you—whole-wheat blueberry pancakes!" Dad calls from the kitchen. I yawn and swing my legs out of bed. My dad's pancakes are delicious. Besides, what else is there to do on a Saturday morning if you aren't dancing?

At the table I notice a colorful brochure tucked under my juice glass. "What's this?" I ask.

Dad is standing at the stove. "Read it and you'll see," he says, flipping a pancake.

I pull out the brochure reluctantly. On the cover it says, *Dance the summer away at Camp Dance.* Below is a picture of a group of girls leaping in the air. I flip through images of happy girls on boats, swimming in a lake, roasting marshmallows and posing in dance costumes.

"Great," I say flatly. "Who's it for?"

Dad flips another pancake and looks at me. "It's for you. The first session starts next week."

"You're kidding, right?" I flick through the brochure again. "There's, like, not a single ballet picture in here."

"Exactly. Just because your ballet program is canceled doesn't mean you can't dance this summer. You'll get to try the cha-cha, tango and jazzy tap-tap."

"Jazzy tap-tap?"

"Here. Look in the brochure." Dad comes over and jabs a finger at the list of dance styles:

contemporary, ballroom, hip-hop, jazz and tap. "See, jazzy tap-tap, it says so right there." He flashes me a smile.

"But Dad," I wail, "I don't do 'jazzy tap-tap.'"

"Aha." Dad brandishes a spatula. "Perhaps you can try the hippity-hop instead."

"That's not funny." I scowl and start cutting my pancakes.

Mom comes into the kitchen carrying an enormous laundry basket of clean clothes. "Would you prefer basketball camp?"

I roll my eyes. "No!"

"How about baseball camp, or soccer?"

"I've never gone to camp, so why would I go now? Just because Tess likes it?" I can't help wrinkling my nose. Tess loves sweaty team sports, anything that involves yelling, cheering and hooded sweatshirts with team logos.

Mom puts down the basket of laundry. "Look, Meg, your dad and I have been planning our trip to Italy for the last five years. We've already bought the airline tickets and reserved the hotels. Since you can't go to ballet school this summer, you have to do something else. It's camp or Nana's."

I pull my long black hair tighter into my hair elastic and suck in my breath. I love my Nana, I really do, but she lives in a one-bedroom apartment and watches TV in Farsi all day. She loves nothing more than to force-feed me rich Iranian food and complain I'm too skinny.

"Can't I just stay by myself?"

"You're fifteen! That's way too young to be alone for two weeks. Look, I tried to find another ballet program, but anything suitable was already full. At least dance camp will allow you to stretch and get some exercise," Mom says. "And Mrs. G recommended it."

I stare at her. "Mrs. G suggested I go to dance camp? Why?"

Mom pulls out her phone and starts scrolling through her messages. "Here's her email. 'Meg might want to try Camp Dance in the Okanagan. It's an intensive dance program that allows dancers to focus on a particular style each session. I think it would be a great way to help Meg broaden her dance horizons and develop her stage presence. Meg's dancing is technically very strong, but to get to the next level she needs to learn to connect with her audience and be less

bound by the rules. See you in the fall, Mrs. G.'"
Mom quietly slips her phone back in her pocket.

I want to run to my room and hide in my closet. Instead, I bite my lip. Broaden my dance horizons? Connect with an audience? What does that mean? I know dancers can always improve, but how does someone get better stage presence? I push my plate away and hide my head in my arms on the table.

Mom sits down next to me. "Don't see this as the end of your ballet career. It's not. It's just a different opportunity. Besides, you might have fun meeting new people."

I look up at her. I've gone to the same ballet school and had the same ballet friends forever. Meeting new people is not one of my strengths. I chew furiously on my lip, but I can't hold back my tears. I bury my head in my arms again. I can't spend two weeks holed up in Nana's apartment, but *camp*? With kids I don't know?

Mom is already talking about things I'll need, like towels and a soap dish. She gets up and wanders into the laundry room, musing about sunscreen.

Dad comes over to the table and sits next to me. He tugs gently on my earlobe. "You'll have a good time. You'll get to try new dancing and lots of other activities." He picks up the brochure. "Look, you can do sailing, Birdie."

I scrunch up my brow at my old nickname. Dad's always called me Birdie because I was such a skinny baby. I'm still thin now, even though I eat whatever I want, but I'm strong from ballet too. I lift my head. "Why would I want to sail?"

"Because it's fun."

"To you, maybe." I collapse back on the table.

Dad taps his finger on the back of my head. "Listen, going to camp is the kind of thing my parents moved to Canada for. I was too old by the time we got here and my parents figured out that kids did these camping things. So please, go and enjoy."

I look at Dad. "Are you done with the guilt?"

"Yes. Go and have fun." Dad reaches out to kiss my forehead, but I bat him away.

Two

I have a secret fear I've never told anyone, not even Julia. I keep hoping it will go away, but that hasn't happened yet. Instead, Mrs. G's email is blowing it up in my face. The truth is, I might not make it as a ballerina. Everyone pretends that I will, that all the years of expensive lessons and costumes and sore muscles will eventually be worth it, but I'm not sure. And Mrs. G's email shows that she has doubts too. How do you develop stage presence? I've never been good at connecting with people. I think about asking Julia, but it's embarrassing, the kind of thing you might talk about with a psychologist or school counselor. I wish I could forget it, but I can't.

As I spend the rest of the weekend packing shorts and T-shirts into one of Tess's hockey bags that still stinks of sweat, I imagine my parents whispering about Mrs. G's email in the kitchen. I focus on the camp list, on finding a flashlight and mosquito repellent and sunscreen and a dorky sun hat. I try not to look at Mom whenever she comes into my room with a raincoat or calamine lotion, so she won't see how ashamed I feel that my secret has been exposed.

To keep myself calm, I focus on the camp brochure like it's the latest fashion magazine. I decide there are some camp activities I might want to try. I'm not into waterskiing, canoeing or ball sports, but yoga, drama and art classes sound okay. Then I read a section on camp rules. I'm not allowed to smoke or drink or bring candy, none of which I care about, but I almost bolt out of bed when I read Camp Dance is tech-free. No cell phones allowed.

How will I ever survive without texting Julia? And it will take me weeks to catch up on *Fashionista* and *Style Rookie*, my favorite fashion blogs. I won't be able to look at the websites of Stella McCartney or Chanel, my favorite designers, for two whole weeks. For a couple of moments I wonder how bad fourteen days at Nana's could be. Very bad,

I decide and flop back on my bed. I send Julia a gloomy text with the latest update.

By Sunday night my duffel bag lurks in my room like a strange body. I haven't packed any tights or tutus or even toe shoes. I wasn't sure what to pack, so I chose the most basic items: three black leotards and some plain workout shorts. I can't imagine wearing the vintage Chanel skirt I just found in a thrift store downtown or my knockoff Prada bag at camp, so they linger in my closet, along with the amazing cream-colored Jean Paul Gaultier dress Mom found for me for 80 percent off.

The only other dance item I've packed is my copy of *Ballet Shoes*. I know it's a kids' book, and I'm way too old for it, but it feels like a teddy bear. I even slept with it for a whole year when I was seven. When I first met Julia, I found out she did the same thing. That's how we became friends.

Julia is a good dancer and, more important, a good person. Some of the girls at ballet are too competitive, and if you get the parts they want, they won't talk to you. Melanie Webster hasn't spoken to me since I got the solo for the recital.

Julia was just happy for me to get the part. She came by this morning to say goodbye and brought me a stash of new fashion magazines, including *Lucky, Vogue, Teen Vogue* and *Elle*, to use in my scrapbook. Mostly I make my collages online on Polyvore now, but since that won't be happening this summer, I've decided my old scrapbook is better than nothing.

* * *

On Monday morning, my parents drop me off for the camp bus. When I see the chaos in the parking lot, I almost can't get out of the car. I'm expecting girls to be calmly lined up, but instead there is a riot of motion: cars honking, kids calling to each other, duffel bags strewn everywhere. Some of the kids are hugging each other like they haven't seen each other in a million years, and other kids are hugging their friends and parents goodbye like they're not going to see them for another million years. Everyone seems to know at least one person, except me. And these girls are different than the ballet girls I know. Not all of them are thin, and some have nose rings and hair dyed in vibrant colors. One of the counselors trying to shoo girls onto the bus has a tattoo of a hawk on her muscular calf. I try to imagine Mrs. G with a tattoo, but I just can't see it.

When the bus starts honking, I finally get out of the car and hand Mom my phone. I make sure to give my parents one final suffering look and an extra-loud sigh before I get on the bus, but they're too excited about their trip to notice.

I take the first seat at the front and reach into my pocket for my phone to text Julia, but my pocket is empty. Behind me, kids are laughing and shouting. The tinted windows reflect my face back at me. I can see the worry in my brown eyes, the tightness in my thin lips. *Great*, I think. *I look really friendly and fun.*

At the last minute, just before the bus pulls out, a boy gets on and sits next to me. My cheeks heat up right away, which is embarrassing, but I'm pretty sure no one else notices.

I don't know any boys. I don't have time to hang out at school the way other kids do, because of ballet. There are boys who dance, but they take different classes, and most of them aren't interested in girls. Sometimes I think about what it would be like to have a boyfriend, someone to hang out with on Saturday nights, someone who would text sweet things to me. I always remind myself that ballet is more important than boys.

Ballet is more important than anything.

I sneak a glance at the boy next to me. He looks about sixteen, with shaggy black hair and a worn T-shirt. I think he's probably what Julia and I call "a halfie." I'm half Iranian, Julia is half Korean, and this guy is half something Asian, maybe Chinese. He's also kind of cute.

Before I can turn back to the window, the boy sticks out his hand. "Since we're going to sit together, we should probably introduce ourselves." He smiles. "I'm Nio. You're new, aren't you?"

"Yes, this is my first time at camp," I say.

"Well, you're going to love it. It's the best." Nio is so excited he's practically bouncing in his seat.

"Really?" I raise my eyebrows.

"Yep. You get to dance for two weeks and nobody, you know, makes fun of you. So, what kind of dance do you do?"

"Ballet," I say automatically.

"Really?" Nio says. "I didn't think Camp Dance did ballet."

"I know."

"So, I don't mean to be rude, but why are you here?"

I twist my ponytail around my fingers. "The summer ballet program I was supposed to attend got canceled, and my parents had already planned a trip to Italy. They needed to send me somewhere."

"Wow, that's, like, years of therapy waiting to happen," Nio says.

"Thanks." I slump in my seat. We've already left the city, and I can only see highways and bridges against the backdrop of the mountains.

"So, what section did you sign up for?" Nio asks.

"What do you mean?"

"When you filled out the registration form, you had to sign up for a dance section. You know, like contemporary or ballroom."

I hesitate. "I didn't fill out any forms. I guess my parents must have..." I imagine Dad choosing "jazzy tap-tap" or "hippity-hop" for me and feel sick to my stomach.

"Oh well, I'm sure you can choose when you arrive. Your section is important, because that's your main dance class every morning."

"What about you?" I ask. "What kind of dance do you do?"

"All of it." Nio smiles. "But I like contemporary best."

I'm about to ask Nio what's so great about contemporary, but he is already standing up. "Time to see who's here," he says and saunters toward the back of the bus.

Three

The bus ride takes forever. I try to keep myself occupied by rehearsing in my head all the dances I've ever learned, starting when I was four and wore a bumblebee costume, all the way up to my last performance in the pink tutu. I can't believe that was only two weeks ago.

Nio comes back to his seat from time to time to tell me about campers from previous years. He says, "Chelsey is back. She sang 'Tits and Ass' from *A Chorus Line* last year." Or "Logan, who is my best Camp Dance friend, got a nose ring!" Or "This girl Jezina from two years ago says she can do a backflip." I pretend to be interested. Mostly I just smile and nod because the bus is so loud. One group of girls belts out "Do-Re-Mi" from *The Sound of Music* until they're overtaken by other girls singing a rap song full of swearing. A counselor asks them to stop, but the bus doesn't get any quieter. I sink low in my seat and try to stick my fingers in my ears without other people noticing.

I'm not good with lots of noise. Dad says being an introverted dancer is weird, but I don't feel shy when I'm dancing. Still, at the end of the day, after being surrounded by other dancers, I want to be by myself. It makes me worry about camp. What if I need to be alone? I'm hoping there's a bathroom with a door that locks.

After four hours of noise, we finally pull off the highway and onto a long road through a grassy field. When the bus stops, I'm the first one off. It's incredibly beautiful in the Okanagan. Living in Burnaby, I'm used to rainy weather and lots of green grass, trees and bushes. Here, I'm surrounded by yellow and brown sun-scorched fields, and in the distance is Kalamalka Lake, glimmering like a blue eye.

I read in the brochure that Camp Dance has ten cabins, a soccer pitch and a baseball diamond, a small beach and a dock area on the lake. I can see the dining hall at the top of a steep hill.

In front of me is the main camp building, which I already know has five dance rehearsal studios and a performance hall with a stage. Everyone from the bus streams into the performance hall, and I follow. At one end of the large open room is a raised platform with a curved edge. I guess that's the stage.

As more campers come in, the room gets noisier and noisier. It's even worse than the bus. I stand to the side as kids start forming groups. In one corner, dancers raise their wriggling fingers higher and higher, yelling, "Jazz hands, jazz hands, jazz hands!" Other kids make a circle around dancers taking turns freestyling hip-hop moves. The kids in the loudest and smallest group drum their tap shoes against the edge of the wooden stage. Nio has joined a quieter bunch of campers copying a counselor who leads them in an elaborate seated dance with their arms waving above their heads.

I want to bolt out of the building. Where is Mrs. Mamdou to play the piano and Mrs. G to bark out commands at a row of silent, serious girls at the barre? I find myself reaching into my pocket for my phone again, but I only find some lint. I'm walking quickly toward the exit when a counselor wearing a hot-pink Camp Dance T-shirt taps me on the shoulder. She's the tall one I noticed earlier, the one with the hawk tattoo. She also has short dark hair, a nose ring and muscled arms.

"Are you Meg Farahni?" she asks over the noise. I nod, and she beckons for me to step onto the porch. The sun makes me squint, but I'm so happy to be away from the noise I don't care. The counselor holds out her hand. "I'm Tara, and you're going to be in my cabin. Welcome." When she smiles, her eyes wrinkle up as if they are smiling too. "Your father called last week to ask about camp and to tell me about you. He says you're a ballerina looking for new experiences."

"Uh, sort of," I say.

"Well, I think you'll find Camp Dance pretty different from your usual ballet classes, but I hope you'll feel welcome. The kids here are very open-minded."

I'm not sure what to say, but it seems rude to say nothing. I swallow and whisper, "I will."

"Great. Now, before we go in and announce cabins, you should choose a main dance section.

Your parents forgot to fill that out on your form. Have you thought about what you want to do?"

I look over my shoulder into the hall. The ballroom dancers have taken over the back of the room, performing something that looks both corny and complicated. There's no way I can do that, or hip-hop, or tap. And what was with that jazz hand stuff? Just then Nio waves at me from his group. They've finished their arm-waving routine and are now watching one of the older campers perform a dance that involves a lot of rolling around on the floor. It's strange but also graceful. I really don't want to go back inside the hall, but Tara is waiting for me to choose. I look at all those strange faces, all those people I don't know, and then I see Nio again. At least he's friendly, and I've met him. "I guess I'll try that," I say, pointing toward Nio's group.

"Contemporary," Tara says. "That's a good choice for a ballet dancer. And I teach that class." She makes a note on her clipboard and waits for me to go inside. I take a deep breath and enter the din of the hall. Luckily, everyone is so busy talking that no one pays any attention to me as I walk toward Nio.

Before I can even sit down, Nio wraps his arms around me, squashing me in a giant sweaty hug, almost knocking me over. "You chose us! We're going to have the best time ever."

I can't help smiling at his enthusiasm.

Four

o calm myself down, I think about tendus. There are seventy-two different ballet steps, but a tendu, the brushing of the foot across the floor until it's pointed to the front, side or back, is my favorite. It's simple but elegant. Some people twiddle their thumbs or gnaw their nails; I do tendus. Since I can't stand up and practice tendus in front of everyone, I imagine myself at the barre while the camp director welcomes the campers, reviews the rules and announces the cabins.

When Tara calls my name, I try to hold my head high as I cross the hall, even though I want to keep my chin close to my chest and scurry out. I follow the other girls, who rush back to the bus to get their stuff and then carry their bags across a field to a row of cabins. Tara helps me with my bag.

When I get to the wooden cabin I understand why the other girls were hurrying. Bunks are chosen by whoever gets to them first. I look around the dim wooden room with its two tiny windows and wooden rafters. Even though everyone has taken off their shoes, the floor feels gritty. The only spot left is an upper bunk right by the door. All the other girls are laughing and talking and unpacking their clothes into the drawers between the beds. Some of the girls tape pictures from their dance recitals to the walls. Tara has the radio playing a Top Forty station. No one talks to me; they're all too busy saying hi to everyone they already know.

I shove my T-shirts and shorts into a shallow drawer, and then I look through my fashion scrapbook for something to decorate the wall. I decide on a series of prom dresses from *Teen Vogue*. Just as I'm taping them up, a girl with short, spiky, dirty-blond hair comes over to talk to me. She's wearing an off-the-shoulder T-shirt with a picture of a car on the front, cut-off denim shorts and a pair of scuffed boots that make her outfit more interesting than any of the other girls' mall-inspired clothing. "Interesting," she says, pointing to the wall. "Everyone else has recital pictures of themselves."

.I'm not sure what to say. "I'm Meg," I finally reply.

"Logan."

"Oh, are you Nio's friend?"

"Yeah, how do you know him?"

"We sat on the bus together."

Logan nods slowly. "He's my best friend here."

"Lucky you." I try to smile. "So you must be in contemporary."

"What else do you know about me?" Logan folds her arms across her chest.

"Um, nothing. I was just going to say that I'm doing contemporary too."

Logan licks her lips. "Great, that's great. Nio and I have already planned some moves."

. "Yeah, I don't really know how to do contemporary yet."

"Then why did you sign up for it?"

"I just, well...I'm not sure." I tug on my ponytail. It seems too complicated to explain to Logan.

She gives me a weird look.

Luckily, Tara chooses that moment to announce that unpacking time is over and everyone is to meet in front of the cabin under the trees. I quickly finish taping the dress pictures and file out with the other girls.

"We're going to have an awesome couple of weeks," Tara says, "because everyone knows Camp Dance is the best!" The girls cheer around me, and I try to smile. Tara continues, "I know almost all of you from previous years, but there are some new faces, and we need to get to know everyone, so we're going to play a couple of quick games. The first one goes like this. I'm Tara and I really like birds." She points to her hawk tattoo, then turns to me. "Repeat my line and then add something about yourself."

I swallow and repeat Tara's line and then add, "So, I'm Meg and I like ballet." I'm relieved to be at the beginning of the game so I don't have to remember much. The other girls' names pass in a blur of favorite songs and singers. Only Logan is memorable because she does karate as well as dance. She also wrinkles her nose when she repeats my line about ballet, which makes me a little uneasy.

I daydream through the rest of the icebreaker games. All I want is five minutes of quiet to think about the day and to worry about contemporary dance. While the other girls play charades, which I suck at because I don't know the musicals they keep choosing, music blasts over the PA system. "Attention, campers! It's dinnertime," a voice rings out. "The first one to the dining hall who can name this song gets to open freestyle tonight!"

"They're playing 'It's a Hard Knock Life' from *Annie*," Jodie, a girl with dark curly hair, squeals. She and her friend Cassidy start racing up the hill to the dining hall. I turn to admire Cassidy's hair, which is long and blond with the tips dyed purple. The other girls saunter up the hill behind them.

"What's open freestyle?" I ask Tara.

"Oh, our evening program on the first night is always a dance showcase. The first person to the dining hall gets to go first." Tara starts walking up the hill.

I follow along beside her, twisting my fingers behind my back. "Does everyone have to dance?"

"No, only if you want to."

I unclench my fists.

Dinner is macaroni and cheese, which everyone is excited about. I'm too nervous to eat much.

At least I don't have to worry about who to talk to, because the dining hall hums with the voices of a hundred kids, mostly girls, all talking at the same time.

After dinner, the other girls dig through their bags looking for costumes, trying to decide if they will dance in the opening freestyle. I lie flat on my bed, trying to block out the sound of my cabin mates.

"I might dance, but then again, I might be too nervous."

"I will if you will."

"Then you have to go first."

"We could do it together, but only if we do that routine—you know, the one that goes like this."

I bury my head in my pillow so the others won't see me sticking my fingers in my ears.

"Okay, time to go—it's seven o'clock." Tara starts bustling everyone out, despite protests that they need one more minute in front of the mirror or need to change one last time. Maybe no one will see me up on my bunk, but Tara pokes her head up by my pillow. "It's showtime!" She holds out her hand to help me down.

Open freestyle is a new kind of crazy. Most of the dancers seem content to get up on stage without choreographed routines and make up a dance on the spot to their favorite song. This is both impressive and terrifying. What if you can't think of what to do next? There are younger kids who do acrobatics, a pair of girls who perform a jazz dance, a bunch of boys who break-dance and then a long series of tap dancers. Jodie and Cassidy tap a musical-theater number they know well, their excitement showing on their faces. Jodie doesn't even seem to care that she slips at the end. She just gets up, bows again and prances offstage.

When I finally crawl into my bunk that night, I'm so tired I could cry. I'm hoping to fall asleep immediately, but my sleeping bag smells weird, and I miss my bed with its pink sheets. I can't stop thinking about the day, about the bus and the hill and the lake and all the noise. I stretch out and point and flex my toes. Tomorrow I'll have to find time to do some ballet exercises; otherwise I'll be really behind when I get back.

Just when I'm starting to fall asleep, I hear someone whisper-yell "Fashion show!" I open one eye enough to see Logan spring out of her bunk wearing a silver tank top and a hot-pink feather boa with her pajama bottoms. She struts the length of the cabin, turns and poses at the bathroom door, then starts prancing between the bunks. The other girls cheer her on. Logan looks ridiculous in her pajamas yet stylish, like she should be in an Alexander McQueen runway show. I'd add a pair of big sunglasses or maybe a checked hat to her outfit.

I'm about to offer my own sunglasses when the cabin door opens and Tara pops her head in. "Busted. Get back to bed." Logan shimmies her way back to bed and I lie staring at the ceiling, wishing it was me who was brave enough to prance around in front of everyone.

Five

I am dreaming of performing a sissonne, a jump from two feet onto one, when a blast of Elvis over the PA system wakes me. I want to bury my head under my pillow to make the music go away. Instead, I get out of my bunk to be first in the bathroom. I dress quickly so I can walk to the dining hall alone, before the other girls get up. It's another beautiful sunny day, the camp grass already drying out. From the hill in front of the dining hall, I can see the lake sparkling and the brown and yellow hills surrounding the water.

The dining hall is quiet this morning, with only the clink of silverware and the scraping of chairs breaking the silence. I make myself a cup of tea and nibble a piece of toast. The other girls from my cabin slowly take their places around the table. "Campers," the director announces over the PA system, "eat a good breakfast, with either an egg or some peanut butter. It's going to be a big morning of dance."

After breakfast and a short cabin cleanup, it's time for the main dance class of the day. I square my shoulders, pull my hair into a ponytail and take a casual look around to see what the other girls are wearing. Most of them have on dance tights and fitted T-shirts or workout tops and shorts. I pull on a black leotard and shorts. At least my clothes won't make me stand out.

I walk slowly across the hot, dry field to the dance studios. Cassidy and Jodie catch up with me and start singing and pretending to do a ballet dance around me. I can't help smiling at their silliness. They're friendly, even if they are kind of immature, and by the time I arrive at the contemporary-dance studio, I feel more relaxed.

The studio has a wall of mirrors and the ballet barre across one wall. I tap my foot against the floor; it will be good for jumps. I take a deep breath, kick off my flip-flops and sit down to stretch, my legs spread wide in a V and my chest resting on the floor.

A few moments later Nio comes in with Logan.

"Whoa." Nio gasps, lifting a hand to his forehead in mock surprise. "Could you be any more flexible?" He sits down beside me and stretches his legs out in front of him, pretending not to be able to reach farther than his knees. I quickly pull my feet together and sit with the soles of my feet touching.

Nio looks up at Logan. "This is the girl I was telling you about. Meg."

Logan looks down at me. "Oh, the ballet girl."

I nod. "Hi."

"Yeah, ballet's cool," Nio says.

Logan scrunches up her face. "It's kinda boring..."

I wish I was the kind of girl who would stand up and show her how amazing ballet is. Instead, all I do is duck my head.

"No, watch this." Nio stands up, clasps his hands to his chest and does a drag step into a leap, followed by a pirouette.

My heart expands. "You do ballet?" I ask.

"I take a few classes for technique." Nio leaps again.

Logan yawns.

"I know that sequence," I say, and I stand up and do a chassé, a quick gliding step with my right foot ahead of my left, into a pose with my head tipped back and my arms over my head.

"That's right." Nio strikes a similar pose.

"Okay, ballet people, that's enough," Logan says.

Nio does a few more moves and then swings away from me. "That was fun," he says.

I smile back. Then Nio and Logan link arms and walk away to practice jumps on the other side of the studio. I wish he had stayed to do more ballet with me.

Other kids of all ages come into the room and start warming up. I stretch, careful not to attract too much attention. Then Tara comes in and begins flipping switches on the stereo. I sigh. Maybe this contemporary thing won't be too bad; at least Tara seems friendly. Tara claps her hands, and the kids, all girls except for Nio and two other boys, stand up and fall into rows. I scurry to the back of the room while Nio and Logan take places at the front. Tara starts the music, a soft, luminous Celtic song. She smiles and reaches her arms above her head in an expansive stretch. The other dancers copy her and so do I.

The warm-up is different from anything I've done before. There are no pliés, no tendus or battements or barre work. Instead, Tara leads a series of reaches, stretches and large sweeping movements. It's all easy, but weird. For one exercise, we contract our stomach muscles, bend our knees, pull in our arms to our chests, and then release in a big stretch, stepping to the side. I can't figure out what the point of it is. It isn't much of a stretch and there's no technique to it. Ten minutes into the warm-up and I haven't even broken a sweat. And the weirdest thing of all, Tara keeps calling out "contract and release" and smiling as if we should be enjoying ourselves. No ballet teacher I've ever had has expected anyone to enjoy the warm-up.

Tara switches the music to something Spanish-sounding and begins an exercise where you have to kick to the side. I let my foot sweep up, perfectly pointed, to my ear. The other dancers only kick to their waists or their shoulders. All eyes turn toward me in the mirror, including Logan's; she scowls at me. I pretend not to notice their stares and decide not to kick that high for the rest of the exercise.

Following the warm-up there is a series of movements across the floor done in twos: turns, jetés and other leaps. I am good at these, my legs in my jeté almost reaching past 180 degrees into an oversplit. I try not to pay attention to the whispers following me. Many of the other kids are good dancers, but no one has my technique. Logan and Nio are among the best dancers in the group. Logan may not be as flexible as me, but she attacks each of the jumps with an impressive energy. I can tell she would be fun to watch onstage. I wonder if that's how Mrs. G wants me to dance.

After the warm-up there is a short break. Everyone drinks from their water bottles, and most of the girls fix their hair. A few of the kids practice a move where you fall from standing into a push-up position. I watch, fascinated. It looks both graceful and dangerous. I want to try it, except not with other kids watching. I'd like to talk to Nio again, but he's sitting with the other boys, so I sit alone, watching.

At the end of the break, Tara gathers everyone together. "Good work, dancers. We're going to have an amazing two weeks in contemporary this year. I know usually we start a routine right away, but this year, you guys are going to be the choreographers, not me." The dancers look around at each other. A few raise their eyebrows. Some of the older kids look excited. I'm not really sure how I feel about this. I've never had a chance to choreograph anything before. I could create a ballet dance easily, but not contemporary.

"In order to get you prepped for choreography," Tara says, "the second half of our class is going to be an improv session. It's a little different, but I think you'll love it. Just be open to experimenting and moving how you feel."

Improv is when you make up your own dance, on the spot. Julia and I have done that a million times before. Still, I cringe a little when I hear Tara say we should move how we feel. That's the part Mrs. G wants me to work on: emotion. The dancers choose positions in the room, and I stand at the back again, not sure what will happen next. Tara turns on a playful song with loud saxophones and shouts over the music, "Okay, dancers. Let's see what you can do. We're going to start with the dance of the happy penguins!

It's a beautiful sunny day in Antarctica, and the snow is slippery. Don't limit yourself to only penguin moves. How do you think penguins feel?"

My eyes open wider. *Penguins? I have to dance like a penguin?* They don't even have proper legs, just feet. All around me, other dancers start to move, most of them waddling joyfully, flapping their hands like little penguin wings. A few hop up and down and bob their heads. Nio runs and slides across the floor on his knees, arms outstretched.

"Dancers," Tara adds, "think about the space around you. Are you going to be low to the ground, or higher in the air?"

I still haven't moved. *Penguins?* But this is why I am here, to experiment, to try new things. I could try a penguin pas de chat, but to happy saxophone music? I back farther away from the other dancers, until I am against the barre. *C'mon, Meg,* I tell myself, *just try.* And so I bend my knees and attempt an awkward penguin plié. *Would penguins stick out their bums when they bend their knees?* Then I do a few battements, kicking my feet in front of me in time to the music, then a rond de jambe, my toe pointed to the floor and moving from the front to the side. I'm about to try a penguin arabesque, with my leg bent behind me instead of straight, when the music changes. The new song is lyrical, with heavy drums. It sounds sinister.

"Penguins, a wind has come up, and clouds are coming in," Tara yells. "There may be a predator in the area." The other dancers become more frenzied. One girl starts to pull at her long hair, her feet moving in a series of small, intense steps. Another boy crawls on the floor, growling as if he is the predator. *Do penguins even have predators?* One smaller girl hops on one foot, clapping her hands. I suck in my breath and try a fast turn on demi-pointe, turning quickly as if to keep away from something scary. I think about my hands and let them flutter nervously around me, keeping time to the music.

Then Tara switches the music to a classical piano piece. "The music has changed and so will you," she calls out. "Now you must dance as if you are the color purple. What does purple feel like to you?"

I stop. *Purple?* It's a color, not a feeling. My mind goes totally blank. The other dancers start to make contract-and-release movements across the floor. I back myself against a wall, watching them. This is too weird. I start edging toward the exit and then flee, down the hallway and into the bathroom.

Six

It's cool and dark in the bathroom. I crouch on a covered toilet seat, my head resting on my knees, and imagine doing pas de valse—a waltz step—to normal ballet music. I'll never be able to do contemporary. All that contract-and-release stuff was weird enough, but pretending to be purple? I close my eyes. Maybe I could bring a book to class and read at the back. Or slip out the door and find a room to practice some ballet exercises. That would be a good use of time.

Except that isn't why I am here. I'm supposed to be learning to be more flexible. Less rule-bound. Before I fled the room, I caught a glimpse of Logan's purple dance. She was swinging her arms around her head as if she was a warrior.

I stretch out my back and then wilt into a slump. *What does purple feel like anyway?* It makes me think of my parents drinking red wine on the back porch in the summer, the clink of the wine glasses. You could do a series of glissades, a sliding step beginning and ending in fifth position: that's what a purple wine night would feel like. The music would be very drawn-out, like the jazz music Mom listens to.

I get up from the toilet and stand in front of the mirrors over the sinks and imagine my parents drinking wine in Italy. I hum a little bit and then attempt a slow purple-wine-night glissade, followed by a measured pas de bourrée, a small stepping movement I usually do en pointe. *Exactly right.* I let myself drop to the tiled floor the same way Tara did during warm-up, contracting my stomach and then wilting in a pile of limbs. It feels good. I stand up and do it again. That's how I feel at the end of a really good ballet rehearsal—like a falling leaf—or a crumpled marionette.

Except it's not how I feel now. I still have lots of energy inside me, like I'm a simmering pot. I couldn't even stay for the whole class because of a stupid color. I usually wear soft pastels, like the pale blue of my favorite ballet sweater, or my pink toe shoes. Purple is the color of Tess's soccer uniform. I wrinkle my nose, imagining those purple jerseys in a dank pile on the laundry-room floor. I lift my hand to my forehead in mock horror, the way Nio did when he saw me stretching. Then I tuck myself into a little ball, hands over my head, as if to avoid the purple laundry. I start moving my feet to the beat I can hear from the tap class next door, little angry steps, still thinking of those purple shirts.

I don't hear the bathroom door open. I'm still crouched over, feet tapping, when Logan says loudly, "Why are you dancing in the bathroom instead of in class?" She holds the door open wide so other girls in the hallway can look in and give me funny looks.

I quickly drop my arms. "I was just stretching," I say, even though it was obvious I wasn't. I walk past Logan, holding my head high.

In the hall outside the studios, sweaty dancers are packing their bags. The bell for lunch is ringing, and campers are heading up the hill to the dining hall. I want to hide in my cabin instead. I step back into the studio to get my water bottle. All the other dancers have left, and only Tara is there.

She sees me and smiles. "Hey, I was wondering where you went. You did really well today."

"I did?"

She turns off the stereo system. "Yeah, you've got beautiful technique, and I was so proud of the way you tried all the exercises. I know you normally only do ballet, so this must have been really different for you."

"But I couldn't do the end," I whisper.

Tara tilts her head to the side. "Who cares? You did more than half, right? And tomorrow you can stay longer and do more improv."

I let my shoulders slump. "I don't think so."

Tara throws her arm around my shoulders. "Oh, c'mon. Just think of all the wild stuff you'll have to show your ballet friends back home."

I cringe, imagining dancing like a penguin in front of Julia and the rest of the junior company.

Tara smiles sympathetically and then pulls herself away from me and does a few silly penguin moves with a goofy grin. "Penguin, right?" Then she skips across the room and leaps in the air, both legs bent. When she lands, she swings her arms over her head and falls into the graceful push-up position the other dancers practiced during the break. "That's a happy penguin to me. You?"

I hesitate for a minute. I think about "Dance of the Cygnets" from *Swan Lake*, which we performed as a finale for the year-end show. I can hear the music in my head as I start the sixteen pas de chat, a series of sideways jumps. I start to smile as I dance the steps.

When I finish, Tara calls out, "Bravo! You can do that in class if that's what you feel. You'll blow the other kids away." Then she grabs me in a headlock and rubs my scalp with her fist, something no ballet instructor has ever done. I can't help smiling as I try to pull away. "C'mon," Tara says. "We're going to miss the grilled cheese sandwiches."

"Hey," I say. "What do you call that move you just did, the one where you fell into the push-up?"

Tara shrugs. "I don't know if it has a name. I think I'd call it a windmill fall because of the arm motion."

I nod. When I turn to leave, I see Logan standing in the doorway, watching us. I'm not sure how long she's been there.

"Hey, Logan," Tara says. "Coming to lunch?"

Logan eyes me carefully, runs her fingers through her sweaty hair and then nods. Tara turns out the lights in the studio and the three of us walk up the hill to the dining hall together.

Seven

The first few days of dance camp pass in a blur of moving bodies and starchy meals. I wake each morning dreaming of pliés or pas de chat, and then I suffer through contemporary class, bending and contracting into new poses, humiliating myself in the improv exercises. I try to pretend I'm a storm cloud, a star or a chair. Even though no one is looking at me when I'm doing these exercises, I still feel self-conscious. Dancing is steps to me, not emotion or imagination. I think about Mrs. G saying I need to make a connection with my audience in my dancing, but I don't really get it.

And what does a star feel like anyway? The doubt Mrs. G has unleashed makes it hard to concentrate. If I can't take my dancing to the next level, what will happen to me? I can't imagine not dancing. I've given up so many things for ballet already: the school choir, Saturday-night movies, visiting Nana in Abbotsford, a trip to New York with some school friends and their moms...the list goes on.

If I don't dance, what will I do with the rest of my life? Without ballet, my life feels like dancing onstage without a costume and makeup.

Sometimes Nio talks to me during breaks in our dance classes. Mostly he hangs out with Logan, who still stares at me whenever I kick higher than the other dancers or when she happens to notice me struggling through an improv exercise. I try my best to ignore her. Some days, when contemporary class gets too strange, I do ballet exercises in the bathroom to calm myself down.

In the afternoons we have swimming, boating or arts and crafts. I make beaded bracelets without enthusiasm and swim in the cold lake. You need a partner down at the dock. The one time I ask Nio to be my partner, Logan glares at me as if I am trying to steal him away. I ask Jodie and Cassidy if I can partner with them after that. When we go down to the boating dock, the other girls fight to take out canoes or sailboats. Nio keeps saying I should try waterskiing. "It's the best feeling," he says. "You fly over the lake."

"No thanks," I always say.

Nio just shrugs and leaves me alone. It's not that I don't know how to water-ski; it's more that I don't want to risk an injury that could end my ballet career. Sometimes I take a rowboat out by myself. Mostly I hang out on the dock, reading fashion magazines and feeling bored. I try doing some ballet exercises in the shade, but too many people stare and Logan snickers.

Each evening a different dance section does a performance. The tappers perform a Broadway-style medley. The musical-theater troupe does a series of shorter numbers. The contemporary dancers haven't started their rehearsals, but already they're buzzing around and forming groups. I try to ignore the excitement. No one has asked me to join them.

My favorite part of the day is the quiet hour after lunch. I work on my fashion scrapbook under the trees or read a magazine on my bunk. It's the only time I can be alone.

One afternoon I'm lying on my bunk looking at some magazines and thinking about a collage I'd like to make when I hear Logan outside the cabin, talking to Jodie and Cassidy. "Hey, this is cool," I hear her say. I don't pay attention until I hear Logan say, "I love the colors in this collage." I bolt upright on my bed and look through my backpack for my fashion scrapbook. It's not there.

I'm getting off my bunk just as Logan sticks her head into the cabin. "Did someone lose a scrapbook?"

"I think that's mine." I point to it in Logan's hands.

"Oh." Logan looks surprised.

"Where did you find it?" I ask.

"Outside under the trees," Cassidy says. "I love your collages."

"Yeah," Jodie adds, "especially the winter one."

Logan looks at the ground.

"Thanks. I guess it must have fallen out of my backpack," I say.

As Logan silently hands me the scrapbook, the pages fan open to the back, where I've glued some photos of myself. "Wait, is that you?" Jodie asks.

"Um, yes." I want to take the book back and scurry up to my bunk, but Jodie, Cassidy and Logan are all staring at the photos of me modeling some ballet costumes and also standing in my favorite outfit: my soft gray leather jacket I got from my parents for my fifteenth birthday, my fuchsia pencil skirt and my high black leather boots.

"You look so great," Cassidy says.

"My friend Julia is a good photographer," I say faintly.

"You should put some of those photos above your bunk," Jodie says.

"Oh, maybe."

"Wait," Cassidy says. "You two"—she points at Logan and me—"should totally do costuming together for the final show. You'd be great."

Logan and I look at each other without saying anything.

"Logan did all our costuming for musical comedy last year," Jodie explains. "She was so good at it."

Logan bites her lip and shifts from foot to foot. I can tell she wants nothing to do with me. "I'll think about it," I say. I've never really thought about costuming before. I shove the scrapbook in my backpack with my magazines.

"Is that all magazines?" Cassidy asks.

"Um, yes."

"Wow," Jodie squeals.

I hold out the backpack. "They were a present from a friend. You can borrow them."

Jodie and Cassidy grab *Elle* and *Lucky* and then head out to the shade under the trees. Logan hesitates, her hand above the bag. "It's okay," I say.

I watch her face twist into a frown. "No thanks." She joins Jodie and Cassidy to look at the magazines with them instead.

* * *

The next afternoon, instead of water activities, the contemporary dancers meet for our first rehearsal for our evening dance performance. The room hums with energy. I hang back, not even bothering to warm up.

It takes Tara several minutes to calm everyone down so she can speak. "I know you all have a million ideas, so I've gone ahead and chosen some music I think you'll love. You guys can form groups of your choice, and you have the afternoon to compose a routine. Tomorrow we'll figure out the sequence of the groups and how to get everyone on- and offstage smoothly."

Even before Tara finishes talking, the dancers are moving toward each other and forming tight huddles, their arms around each other. Nio joins with the two other guys and three older girls, including Logan. He beckons for me to join them, but I shake my head. I'm relieved that someone wants me in their group, but there's no way I can dance like them.

Tara puts on the music, a haunting piece with French lyrics that builds in intensity. The song begins with only a woman singing, then adds more instruments and becomes faster until it sounds almost frantic. Then the music stops suddenly and the woman's voice comes back for a few more bars of music. Some of the dancers begin moving to the song, but most of the kids are still taking it in. Some even look like they're holding their breath.

Tara lets a moment of silence pass for us to absorb the music before she speaks. "I knew that would blow you away," she says. Then she nods, and the room explodes with activity as everyone starts talking and moving, except me. Tara runs around with a clipboard, writing down group names.

I'm thinking this is a good time to leave. I'm making my best effort with the improv, but I can't imagine making up choreography or performing contemporary yet. I'm about to slink away when Tara calls my name. "Trying to slip out, were you?"

"I was just going to the bathroom."

"Exactly. Look." Tara shows me the clipboard. "Nio's group already wrote down your name. They need you."

I look over at Nio's group. One of the boys is showing the group a contract-and-release movement that includes the windmill fall. Logan glances at me and then quickly turns away. I frown. "I can't do that. I'll stick out."

Tara taps her foot on the floor. "Okay, fine. You can do a solo."

"What?"

"A solo. The last thirty-two counts of the music, when there's just that voice—you get that. I'll let the other groups know."

"But..."

"No buts. It'll be fantastic. You choreograph it whatever style you want—ballet, contemporary, a twist of the two. There's no improv, so there's nothing to be scared of."

I blush. I'm not really scared of improv. I'm just not good at it. From the corner of my eye, I see Logan watching me. She turns back to her group, but not before rolling her eyes.

I clench my fists. Maybe I *will* do the solo, if only to show Logan what I can do. "Fine," I say. "I'll do the solo, but I'm not practicing here."

Tara shrugs her shoulders. "Suit yourself."

I slip out of the studio and into the empty hallway.

Eight

I slump to the bathroom floor and listen to the music coming from the studio. A solo? *Great.* More unneeded attention. Why did I agree to do it?

My part is only a few bars, enough to slowly enter the stage to that haunting voice and perform a short routine. I get up off the floor and start with some slow pirouettes and then add an arabesque to show off my long lines. What if I contract into that tight spin Tara showed us yesterday? I try it and then add a series of chaînés, simple turns. Contemporary dance has a lot of floor moves, a lot of rolling around, so I add an arched back pose. I finish up with some grande jetés en tournant, jumps with a turn. I add a few of my best ballet moves that I can do without toe shoes so Logan will see some of my technique.

Since the whole choreography takes me only twenty minutes, I spend the rest of the time doing ballet exercises in the bathroom, using the counter as a barre. I pretend Mrs. G is counting out the steps. I can hear her voice calling out corrections—arms soft, back straight—but then I hear her voice telling me I need to be more expressive if I want to make it to the next level. She means the senior company. I've got one more year in the junior company to prove myself. If I don't make it to the senior company, that's the end of my ballet career. Only dancers from the senior company go to national auditions.

I try to imagine what my life would be like if I didn't dance. I would just be a girl. No one special. A lump grows in my throat. I've always thought that if I practiced hard, I could make it. I have no idea how to be more expressive or connect with an audience. A few tears well in my eyes. I have to make it. I ball my fists with determination and swing my leg out in a wild turn.

The bathroom door opens just as I'm spinning out of control. "Stretching again?" Logan asks.

I stop abruptly and tuck my hair back into my ponytail. "Actually, I was perfecting my solo." My voice shakes a little, but I can't help sounding proud.

Logan's face flushes. "What, just because you're some skinny ballet girl you get a solo? That's so unfair."

I could tell Logan it's because I don't know how to do contemporary, but I just lift my chin a little and pretend to practice even though I'm only doing a pirouette.

Back in the studio, Tara calls all the dancers together to show each other their routines. I sit at the back and watch. Each group has created a dance that reflects the music—some lyrical pieces for the slower parts of the song, and others charged with energy for the most intense part of the music. Every dance is better, more passionate, than the last. I start hoping Tara will forget about me, or that we'll run out of time. My stupid routine is just steps I've put together, without any emotion. If I get up and perform my pirouettes, it'll look stiff and fake. Mrs. G knows what she's talking about.

I fold my legs up to my chest and wrap my arms around them. Logan can have my solo.

When Tara asks me to come up to the front, I say, "I'm not done yet."

She hesitates and then nods her head. "You'll show us tomorrow."

The dinner bell rings and I'm the first one to leave. Outside, girls are calling to each other on their way back from swimming or boating. For once I'm happy to be surrounded by their noise instead of the thoughts in my head.

In the dining hall, Logan sits at the other end of the table and sends me murderous glances. Then she turns to the girl sitting next to her, and I can tell she's talking about me. I pick at the chicken nuggets on my plate, but I'm too anxious to eat. When Tara isn't looking, I slip out the back door as if I'm going to the bathroom. Instead, I wander through the cherry orchard behind the dining hall. The scent of dishwashing soap and the clash of pots and pans waft out of the building. I pick a handful of cherries from a low branch and settle under a tree.

Why does Logan care so much that I got the solo? She's just like Melanie Webster back home—jealous. I rub my temples. If only Logan knew there was no reason to be envious.

Nio comes out of the dining hall and starts walking toward me. "Hey, I wondered where you went."

I shrug. Nio sits down next to me and starts tugging on some grass. "I know Logan is being really awful. She's just not a ballet person."

"I'm not a contemporary person and I`m not awful to her," I shoot back.

"Yeah, but it's different. Logan's here on scholarship. She doesn't get to take ballet, or other dance classes either, because her mom can't afford it."

"Oh. So she gets to be mean because she's poor? That sounds really fair."

"She's not that bad," Nio says.

I raise my eyebrows at him.

Nio slumps against the tree. "Look, she's my best friend. Our first summer here, we were both on scholarship and didn't know anyone, so we promised to stick together. Logan included me in everything, even though I was the only boy our age at camp."

"So even if she's being mean, you're still going to stand by her?"

"Well, I do tell her to relax every now and then."

"Great," I say. "You can tell her to relax about my stupid solo."

"Ooh," Nio says. "I can't wait to see it."

"Don't hold your breath," I mutter.

Nio gets up to go back into the dining hall. "You coming?"

I shrug. "Don't wait for me."

* * *

I have a hard time falling asleep that night. I keep thinking of the way Logan glared at me. When I finally do sleep, I dream I am onstage dancing. First I fall out of a pirouette, wobbling out of control; then I'm stumbling through a pas de chat. When I attempt the windmill fall, I wake with a sweaty start just before I crash to the floor.

Nine

In the morning I leave the cabin early and get to the studio before anyone else. Maybe, if I think carefully, I can fix my solo. I have thirty-two counts to show what I can do, to figure out how the music makes me feel. I pace around the room, lips pressed together. I remember how the song builds and builds and then crashes. I decide it feels like waking up the day after a big performance and being disappointed it's over.

I start with the pirouette from yesterday and try to make my arms show my sadness. Then I sink to the floor as if a heavy weight is pushing me down. When I roll over into the arched-back pose, I realize Logan and Nio are standing at the door, watching me. I freeze. "What are you guys doing here so early?" I ask.

"We wanted to talk about ideas for next week's choreography," Nio explains.

"Is this your solo?" Logan smirks.

I close my eyes and wish they'd disappear. "Yes."

"Cool," Nio says. "Can you show us?"

"No," I say, still lying on the floor. "You'll just make fun of me."

"Why would we do that?" Nio asks.

"Because it's terrible," I say.

Logan drifts to the side of the room. "I don't think it's fair for anyone to have a solo."

Nio ignores her. "Show me what you've got so far. Maybe I can help."

I hesitate for a moment, then take a deep breath. What's the worst thing that can happen? Logan makes more fun of me? I think I can deal with that. I perform the short routine, rushing through the movements. "See? It's awful," I say when it's over.

Nio frowns. "It's not awful, it just doesn't make sense yet. It's the sad part at the end, right?"

"Yeah, the lonely bit."

"Okay, so we have to make your dance look lonely."

Logan walks back over to us. "Here's what *I* would do." She whips herself into the pirouette, and then, instead of falling to the ground, she hurls herself to the floor as if she's been hit by a comet. She changes my arched pose into a sweeping leg motion on her back that pushes her to standing. She runs a small circle, her arms reaching out as if to grab someone, before she does the jetés. Then, her face filled with anguish, she performs a tight spin, her arms covering her head.

I stare for a moment. Logan can do what Mrs. G wants me to do: she can make an audience feel a dancer's emotion. She made *me* feel it. "How did you do that?" I ask her.

Logan shrugs. "I don't know. I just like making things up."

"That was amazing." I stand up slowly and try to copy Logan's routine. I feel silly throwing myself to the floor and whipping my legs in the air, but I'm starting to feel the desperation I want to show. When I'm done, I look over at Nio. "How was that?"

Nio nods. "Better."

Logan throws up her hands. "Now I'm choreographing your piece for you? Great. I don't understand why you even got a solo!"

"Look," I say, "it's because I don't know how to do contemporary. At least, not yet."

"So why are you even here?"

"I'm here to learn new dance styles, broaden my horizons." *So just be nice to me*, I think.

"Broaden your dance horizons? What does that mean?"

"It means..." I turn a pirouette. "It means I suck."

Nio says, "Look, whoever said you suck obviously has no idea what they're talking about. You're the best dancer ever."

Logan rolls her eyes. "I'm going to fill up my water bottle."

I cringe as she stomps out of the studio.

"Forget about her," Nio says. "Do the routine again."

Logan's dance doesn't feel as awkward the second time.

Nio nods when I finish. "Good," he says. "Now could you do it with more snap?"

"Snap?"

"You know, put more energy into your moves. It looks kind of...correct right now."

I tug on my ponytail. "Correct is what I know."

Nio thinks for a moment. "What if when you're doing the moves, you pretend you're kicking the crap out of someone?" He pretends to punch someone in the stomach.

"I've, uh, never really done that," I say.

Nio grins. "What, no younger brothers?"

"Just a sister."

"Okay," Nio says. "Pretend there's a rubber wall you're trying to knock down." He flails out his leg again and brings one fist up to punch the air.

I kick, trying to imitate him. I feel ridiculous, but a sizzle of energy runs down my limbs.

"Okay, now put that in your face too. Show the anger you feel."

"Anger?"

"Yeah, like you want to try to hurt me." Nio bounces around me like a boxer.

"I don't know..."

"Okay, how about this?" Nio minces around me on his toes, his face scrunched into a little pout. "Ooh, ballet," he says, pretending to be Logan.

I kick my leg out in developpé, as if kicking at Nio. Then my fist comes out. Nio turns toward me just as I swing, and my hand cracks hard against his shoulder. "Oh my god, I'm so sorry," I say, shaking my hand.

Nio grins. "No you're not."

"No, not really." I am nervous and excited at the same time. I run across the room to get away from Nio and jump into a jeté, and my limbs split with energy, the way I want them to. I like the look on my face in the mirror too.

"That's it," Nio says. "Now do that in your dance."

I perform the routine once more and it starts to feel more natural, like it's part of me. I take a deep breath. Maybe I *can* do contemporary. Or at least this solo.

Other dancers start entering the studio, along with Logan.

"How's your solo?" she says with a sneer.

"Much better." I pause and take a deep breath. "I know you didn't want to help me, but you really did. If you ever want, I'd be happy to help you."

"With what?" Logan asks.

"I don't know. Maybe your technique," I say.

"That would be great," Nio says.

"What's wrong with my technique?" Logan starts walking toward me.

I step back until I'm against the barre.

Logan raises a fist. "Just kidding," she says, but she isn't smiling. Then she spins away.

Nio shakes his head. "That's just Logan."

* * *

Tara starts class a few minutes later. She leads a shortened warm-up, and then each group performs again. At the end of each performance, everyone claps, and Tara and some of the older dancers make suggestions. Nio and Logan's group is the last to dance. Set to the most intense part of the music, their choreography, a fast-paced series of turns, leaps and angular movements, ends with the dancers lying flat on their backs, arms and legs spread, as if they've been shot.

"Great," Tara says. "You guys can still be onstage when Meg comes on and performs her solo." She turns to look at me. "Ready?"

I start to sweat. I stand up, shake out my arms, crack my toes and start the slow pirouettes, without the music. I count in my head as I fall to the floor and then whip my legs into the air. When I finish the routine, the dancers whisper among themselves. Tara nods and says, "Looks good. Okay, let's do it with the music."

I wait at the side of the room while the other dancers perform their routines. I look at Logan; she refuses to look back at me. When the voice begins, I start moving across the floor. For a few minutes I forget about the girls watching me, and that I'm doing a pirouette on demi-pointe in bare feet, and what Mrs. G would think about my mixed-up routine.

When the music ends, I sit up and blink at the girls in front of me. Nobody moves or claps. They just stare. Finally an older girl says, "That was the craziest thing I've ever seen." The other dancers nod and smile. When I look over at Logan, jealousy bubbles up from the tight frown on her face.

"I've got goose bumps from that," Nio yells. "It was amazing."

"Logan and Nio really helped me with the choreography," I say.

Tara beams at me and then at Logan and Nio. "Great. I love when dancers work together."

Nio raises his hand for a distance high five, but Logan presses her lips together so tightly they disappear. Still, I don't let that dampen the smile starting to spread across my face.

* * *

We spend the rest of the rehearsal bringing the groups together and discussing costuming. I perform my finale a few more times, adding in some of Tara's suggestions. Before Tara dismisses everyone, she announces a meeting tomorrow after dinner for anyone who wants to choreograph for the final performance of Dance Camp. I don't pay much attention, but I notice Logan and Nio exchanging glances.

By the time the dinner bell rings, I am hungry and sweaty and genuinely excited. And later, after dinner, I'm not all alone lying on my bunk. Instead, I'm one of the girls searching for the right black leotard and vying for mirror space to apply sparkly eye shadow. I use the black lipstick all the other contemporary dancers wear even though it means sharing the same tube.

Waiting to go onstage, I feel my familiar performing excitement rise when the music comes on and the first dancers start to move. My heart fires along to the beat of the music. Then it's my turn to go onstage, and happiness flows through me for the first time since I came to dance camp. The final spin to the floor when the music ends is like diving off a cliff—it's that exciting. I bow with the other dancers as the audience claps, and then I practically skip off the stage, beaming with delight.

Ten

The next morning is Saturday, and the wake-up call doesn't sound until after nine. Breakfast is buffet style in the dining hall, and I sigh with relief when I realize all dance sessions are optional. I spend the morning down at the swimming dock with Jodie and Cassidy, and the afternoon under the trees outside the cabin. At night there's a dance in the main hall.

The evening is warm, with a breeze coming off the lake. The clear night sky sparkles with stars. Everyone else must have known there'd be a dance, because they've brought short skirts and high-heeled sandals. I try not to stare at the other girls dusting their cleavage with sparkles and pulling tight miniskirts over their hips. I only have a cheap navy sundress my mom threw in at the last minute. It hangs from my thin shoulders like I'm a clothesline. I think about the cream-colored Jean Paul Gaultier dress that I rarely have a chance to wear. It's a one-shoulder dress draped in layers of ruffles. It would have been perfect tonight with the Jimmy Choos my aunt sent me for my birthday.

In the hall, streamers hang from the rafters and crepe-paper flowers decorate the walls. A disco ball sheds patches of silvery light around the darkened room, and the girls bounce to the pulsating beat of Beyoncé. I stand awkwardly at the side, watching Logan, Jodie and Cassidy swivel their hips as if they're in a music video. I've started moving toward the back of the room, heading for the balcony, when Nio bounds through the door. "You look like you're leaving, but we haven't danced yet," he says.

I look at the way the other girls are moving. I can't imagine dancing with Nio like that.

He takes my hand and puts it on his shoulder, making me so nervous I bite the inside of my cheeks. "I went to the ballroom-dance session this afternoon, and I learned some new moves. Shall we?" Without waiting for my response, he takes my other hand. A line of nervous shivers runs down my back, even though I know Nio isn't interested in girls. I've done ballet with boys before—I learned the "Peasant" pas de deux from *Giselle*—but I've never actually had a boy ask me to dance. Not outside a studio. Not just because he wants to.

Nio starts guiding me in a circle. "Did you know this is the fox-trot?"

"I didn't." I will myself not to step on his feet. He's wearing a white long-sleeved shirt and dark pants, and his hair is slicked back. He spins me out of his arms, then whips me back in and dips me. We laugh, and then he does it again. I hope Logan sees the whole thing.

"You learned a lot today," I say, grinning.

"Actually," Nio says, dancing us out the back door to the balcony, "my mom has been teaching me ballroom for years."

"Is she a good dancer?"

"Yeah, she used to dance a lot before she had me."

"So she's cool with you dancing and all?"

"Yeah, she's cool. She gets it."

I nod. "And your dad?"

Nio shrugs. "He is now."

The balcony is empty and dark except for the light of the stars. Nio spins me once around the perimeter and then we stand looking down at the lake. I think we're alone until I hear a voice behind me.

"So here you two are," Logan says. It sounds like an accusation. She's wearing a tight pink dress with rhinestones around the low neckline, matching pink sandals and thick-winged eyeliner. Her hair has some electric blue streaks in the front. She looks amazing, like she should be on a runway.

"We were checking out the lake," Nio says. "I'm glad you're here too, because I want to talk to both of you."

Logan narrows her eyes. "Talk to us about what?"

"I've decided it would be great for Meg to be in our final performance group."

Logan arches one eyebrow. "Um, I don't mean to be rude, but you can't be serious."

I pull myself up taller. "Don't worry about it," I say to Logan. "I don't want to be in your group anyway."

Nio grabs my hand. "No, I saw the way you danced yesterday. You're one of the best dancers at camp. We need you."

I soften, even though Logan is glowering at me.

"But we haven't done the choreography yet," Logan says to Nio. She turns to me. "It's not going to have any ballet, so you won't want to be in it."

Nio says to Logan, "You did such a good job fixing up Meg's solo that I thought it would be great if you worked together again."

Logan frowns. "Yeah, I don't think so."

"Oh c'mon." Nio tugs on Logan's hand. "It'll be interesting. What, you're not jealous, are you?"

Logan rolls her eyes. I can see how jealous she is, and it makes me really want to be in the group, if only to show her what I can do. Before I can stop myself, I say, "I'll do it."

"You will?" Nio says.

"Yes."

"Great." Nio raises his hand for a high five, and I slap it. Then he squishes both Logan and me toward him, accidentally banging our heads together. I can smell Logan's hair product. "Oops!"

Nio cries out. Then he leaps away from us to go dance with Jodie and Cassidy.

Logan and I stand staring at each other. "You don't even know what his dance is about, do you?" she says.

"What do you mean *about*?"

"It's contemporary dance, so there's a concept."

"Oh," I say. "I'm sure whatever he's planned will be interesting."

Logan nods. "I'm not sure you'll be able to do all the moves."

A niggle of doubt starts to form in my mind. I try not to let it show. "Well, ballet does give you a strong foundation. I'll try my best." I can't help enjoying my snarky tone.

Logan leans against the balcony railing. "So, tell me what's so great about ballet."

I shrug. "Everything. I love the costumes and the music and the dancing."

"And you're going to be a ballerina?"

I hug my arms around myself and smile, my fingers crossed under my arms so Logan can't see. "Yes," I say.

She juts out a hip, her arms crossed against her chest. "What if you don't make it?"

"What do you mean?"

"I mean, what if you don't get the parts? Or you get injured?"

"That's not going to happen." I hear my voice becoming defensive.

"But it might."

I don't say anything.

"Look, I'm not trying to be mean," Logan says, even though I can clearly hear the cruelty in her voice, "but not everyone makes it. What if there are girls better than you—you know, someone with your technique but who also has fantastic stage presence?"

"I will make it," I say quietly, even though Logan's words make my stomach ache. "If I had my toe shoes here, I'd show you how I can dance."

Logan raises her eyebrows. "I guess we'll just have to wait and see." Then she turns and struts back into the hall. I see her join some of the girls from our cabin under the disco ball. She shoots me one last look, tossing her head before she begins twirling with her arms over her head.

Eleven

Nio waves at me when I enter the dining hall for breakfast, but since he's sitting with Logan, I head for the other end of the table. I eat alone and then warm up at the back of the contemporary studio by myself. Contemporary doesn't seem as weird anymore; it's just something I have to get through. Only five more days of this, and I can go home. Home to my own bed and my own room. Home to Julia.

I started writing a long letter to Julia last night after I left the dance. It was all about how great ballet is going to be this year and which dance companies we should audition for in a few years. I started crying as I wrote because I really wanted to tell her how worried I am about not making it and how my life feels like a vast hole without ballet. Everyone at home is probably improving while I'm wasting my time at stupid Camp Dance.

I follow Tara through the warm-up, stretching, contracting and releasing. I can't be bothered to hold back, and I kick my leg as high as it can go, ignoring the other dancers' attention. I catch Logan's annoyed look and make sure to put as much passion into my kicks as I can. I could compose a whole dance fueled by Logan's sneers.

After the warm-up Tara gathers everyone at the front of the studio. "As I said, you are going to be the choreographers this week. Over the weekend, dancers who wanted to choreograph presented their ideas and music to me. Today, the five choreographers will present their dance concepts to you. Then you'll write down your first three choices, and I'll make the groups. Each group can have three to seven dancers, so there will be a space for everyone. Okay?"

I pull my knees up to my chest. I should have asked Nio what his dance was about before agreeing to be in his group.

Tara nods to one of the oldest girls. "Olivia, why don't you start?"

Olivia stands in front of the group and tucks a loose strand of hair into her ponytail. She cracks her toes against the floor before she begins. "My dance is called *Beware*, and it's about eating disorders. It starts with a group of dancers moving together, and then one girl breaks off and starts dancing by herself. It's kind of a lonely dance, very proud, like she's a swan among ugly ducklings. Her dance is really alluring, and she slowly leads one girl after another toward her. Eventually, almost all the girls are drawn into the eating-disorder dance, except for one. This girl dances a solo, a happy, kind of independent dance, and manages to draw the girls back to her."

Olivia moves to the stereo and plays the Beatles' "Here Comes the Sun." The upbeat song seems at odds with her story. I cock my head to the side. Maybe the difference between the two will make it interesting.

I listen intently as the other dancers move to the front of the room and describe their dance concepts. Not all of them are as detailed as the first. The youngest girl's dance is a day at an amusement park, including a section on a roller coaster and another in a house of horrors.

She demonstrates some of the moves for the different rides, and everyone laughs. Another girl describes a complicated love triangle set to classical music. Then Nio gets up to present his idea.

"My dance is about fear, and learning to conquer it," he says. "And trying new things. It's about facing your fears."

A dance about fear? I feel my face heat up. Is this why Nio wanted me in the group? I look carefully at him, but his face doesn't show anything other than genuine enthusiasm for his dance. I shift on the floor. A dance about fear might be the best choice for me, but it also feels the most dangerous.

Nio says, "I haven't started any choreography because I want it to be a group effort. I'm planning on doing some improv exercises to start." I groan—*more improv?*—and Nio goes on. "I'm looking for dancers interested in working together. I've chosen some music already." He pushes *Play* on the stereo, and the pulsating sound of drums pounds into the room so loudly that it makes me want to leave. The music plays on forever. I want to hide my head under my arms.

I don't have to be in Nio's group. I could write down the name of Olivia's dance on the paper Tara has passed me. I know enough dancers who have suffered from eating disorders. But I know what Mrs. G wants from me. That's why I'm here—to become more expressive. To learn how to make the audience feel something.

And I want to show Logan what I can do. I take the paper that Tara hands to me, and I write down *fear.*

Twelve

ara figures out the groups while one of the
older girls leads the across-the-floor section
of the class. As soon as Tara has the results,
she tapes them to the mirror. Dancers crowd
around the paper and then scatter into groups
across the room. I don't even bother looking
at the lists. Instead, I slowly join Nio in the far
corner. He's sitting on the floor with Logan,
in front of a sheet of paper and some markers.
I avoid looking at Logan at all, and she focuses on
the other three dancers in the group. They are all
serious-looking and slightly younger girls.

"So," Nio begins, "first we're going to start
with a list of things that scare us. Then we'll do
some improv around that. Uh, well, I guess I'll
start." He uncaps a pen. "I'm terrified of spiders."

The other girls laugh and then join in with their own fears. One girl is scared of the dark; another fears public speaking. Everyone laughs when Logan says she fears sex-ed class. I sit listening, flexing and pointing my toes in front of me.

"How about you, Meg?" Nio asks.

"Oh, I'm absolutely terrified of heights," I lie. "Um, especially on roller coasters."

Logan looks up at me, one eyebrow raised.

"We could also put down waterskiing," Nio says.

I glare at him and cross my arms tightly across my body. Some people don't know when to give up. "I'm not scared of waterskiing, just not interested." I try my best to sound bored with the whole exercise. Around us, the other dancers are already running through their routines.

After a few minutes of brainstorming, Nio stands up. "Let's try some improv exercises around some of our fears now. I'll go first, and Logan promised she'd join me."

The other dancers look relieved, and I feel a little better.

"Are we going to start with spiders?" Logan asks.

Nio shrugs. "Sure." He chooses some music and starts moving to a rap song. I watch as Logan pretends to battle an enormous spider, chopping with her fists and kicking it karate-style. Nio does a little two-step, edging his way around a scurrying spider.

When it's my turn, I stand up reluctantly. I'm not really scared of spiders, but I'm not fond of them either. I can pretend, right? Nio chooses a moody-sounding blues song. I start backing away from an imaginary spider and brushing my hands down my thighs. I repeat the movement and add a head-twisting motion as if brushing spiders out of my hair.

I'm almost disappointed when Nio turns down the music. *Okay.* I tap my fingers on the floor. *Let's start the choreography.* I can suggest the two moves I made up in my improv.

But no, Nio isn't done. "This time," he continues, "we're going to dance in pairs. You're going to pretend your partner is whatever you fear most. Your partner will be dancing with you, but also reacting to you." He brushes his hair out of his eyes and turns on the drum music he played earlier. "We'll try it as a group and then we'll present to each other," he says.

Nio chooses to work with one of the other girls. The other two younger dancers pair off, and I find myself staring at Logan.

"I guess we're going to dance together," I say.

"Great," Logan says sarcastically.

The drums start pounding, and I'm not sure how to move. I said I was scared of heights, so I pretend to be up on a building, walking along the edge of it, teetering, and then flattening myself against a wall. *And Logan is supposed to represent that fear? She's a building? Hmm, tricky.* I start stepping away from Logan as if she's dangerous. Meanwhile, Logan appears to be pretending I'm a spider and is backing away from me. We're getting farther and farther away from each other, until I'm almost in another group's space. When Nio turns off the music, Logan is flat against the wall. I cringe, thinking about having to repeat this dance for the others.

Nio and his partner perform first. Nio's dance is small and intricate, with fear seeming to radiate from within him. The two other girls fight a mock battle, their eyes shooting daggers of hate at each other. It's fascinating to watch. Maybe Nio will choreograph something similar for the group, something charged with energy.

When Logan and I stand up to dance, energy seems to fizzle from the room. Logan focuses on her own moves, not even looking at me. I find myself backing farther away. I turn some purposefully teetering pirouettes and then struggle to go on. I add the headshaking movement I came up with earlier and keep repeating it until the music ends. I don't dare look at anyone as I sit back down.

The lunch bell rings soon after we finish. When the other dancers start filing out of the studio, Nio grabs Logan and me by the arms. "Not so fast," he says. He waits until the room is empty. "What was that about?"

"What?" I say.

"Your dance."

I blink. "It was my dance of fear."

"And you?" Nio turns to Logan.

"I was dancing," she protests.

"Pathetic!" Nio yells, his eyebrows rising in disbelief. "What's going on with you two?"

"Nothing," Logan says.

"Yeah right." Nio puts his hands on his hips. When I don't say anything, he says, "Well?"

"Nothing," I repeat. "Are we going to start choreography tomorrow?"

Nio frowns. "I'm not sure."

"The other groups are getting way ahead of us," Logan says, and I nod.

At least we agree on this.

Thirteen

t rains that afternoon, so instead of boating and swimming, we get a choice of dance classes—a hip-hop class on popping, as well as sessions on lyrical jazz, swing and tango. In the evening we watch *Dirty Dancing*. I've already seen it, and my mind keeps wandering back to our unstarted choreography. I caught a glimpse of Olivia's group today. They've learned at least half of their dance already, and it looks great.

The next morning we're back in the studio in our same corner. "So," Nio says, all smiles. "Today we turn yesterday's improv into choreography. To help refresh our memories, I thought we'd do one more exercise, this time to the music." He nods at us all enthusiastically, as if yesterday's session was a huge success. "And instead of thinking about a specific fear, we'll dance a more general feeling of fear, okay?"

Despite his smiles, Nio doesn't sound as confident as he did yesterday. Still, everyone nods, and when he starts the music we all find a spot to dance.

The drums start to pound, and I try to ignore the other dancers around me. I'm not sure how to start. I do a few small jumps to the music to warm up, leaping in first position. I used to think battement developpé was scary, because you might tip over. And before I know it, I'm doing developpé in time to the music, my right foot sliding up my left leg to the knee and then straightening out in front, then to the side and finally into arabesque in the back. It feels good, familiar, but also different to be doing it to the drum music.

When the music ends, I realize all I've done is developpé. Nio did say to do something we feared, and I used to fear them. That should be good enough.

The younger girls dance first this time. They perform an intricate fighting routine. "It's not really improv anymore," one of them explains, "because we practiced it yesterday afternoon."

Nio beams with delight. "Awesome," he says. "That's exactly what I'm looking for." Then he turns to me. "How about you, Meg?"

"Well, I sort of did some ballet moves."

"No problem," Nio says. "We can try to incorporate those into our dance."

I see Logan glowering as I stand in front of the others. I take a breath as the music starts and try to remember why I was scared of battement developpé. I was worried I would fall over if I got my leg too high. Maybe I could play that up. I stand on relevé as I bring my foot to my knee, steady at first, my leg coming up to the front, up to my shoulder. When I release the leg for the second developpé, out to the side, I start to tilt and only let my leg come up to my waist before toppling off-balance. I repeat the movements to the back, each time my leg getting lower, my tilt more dangerous. I try to make sure my face shows increasing fear.

Nio claps when I sit back down. "That was interesting," he says.

"Except not all of us can do that," I hear Logan grumble as she stands up to take her turn. She waits for the fast part of the music to come on and then begins a series of rapid-paced angular moves with her arms, first above her head and then by her sides, her hands flipping up and down and then hovering at her waist. I clench my fists as I watch her. I doubt I'll be able to keep up.

"Okay," Nio says when she finishes. "I think we're making some progress. Let's teach each other some of our moves, and then we'll choreograph them together."

We start with the younger girls' fight dance, and although I think it would be perfect if I could dance with Logan, since we're always fighting, Nio teams up with her and I work with one of the other girls. The moves aren't difficult. We circle each other like panthers and throw pretend punches in alternating patterns. There's a part where we touch each other's shoulders and pretend to wilt to the ground, only to spring up suddenly and execute a bunch of little kicks. I can feel the group relax as we get the steps down.

Then it's Logan's turn to teach. We stand in a row behind her and try to keep up. She goes too quickly, but I don't want to be the one who asks her to slow down. I can see her watching me in the mirror as I struggle, one step behind the others.

"It's actually much faster than this with the music," she says.

When the others have mostly learned Logan's dance, Nio says, "Great, I think we're really moving forward. Meg, are you ready?"

I step to the front and look at everyone. "So, it's just three moves. Right foot comes to retiré." I lift my foot to below my knee and then extend it in front in developpé. "Then it comes to retiré and out to the side, and then to the back." I demonstrate. "Each time, we tilt more to the side and the leg gets lower." I start out with a lower leg height so everyone can do the move.

Everyone copies me, and no one says anything about the fear part being a bit weak. Then Logan says, "Are we sure we want some random ballet moves in our dance?"

"Well, we don't have to—" I start.

"What if we did it with a flexed foot?" Nio suggests, and I smile gratefully. We try it again, with flexed feet this time, and it does look better.

"Oh wait, I have an even better idea," Logan says. "What if we really fall?" She does my move again, but this time her arms come up over her head and she falls into a push-up position. It's the same windmill fall kids were practicing in class last week—the dangerous-looking move where it looks as if you'll slam into the floor but you catch yourself at the last moment.

Nio and the other girls try the move, and the way they're doing it one after the other looks amazing. But I can't do that fall—and from the triumphant glance Logan sends my way, I can tell she knows it.

"That's actually not what I had in mind," I say. "My idea is about the fear of falling, not about actually falling." My voice comes out snootier than I want it to.

"Who cares?" Logan says. "Everyone knows falling is scary. In fact, I think it would be awesome if that was a repeating theme in the dance."

The other girls practice the fall again and again, winding their arms up from my graceful developpé into Logan's brutal fall.

Nio claps his hands. "I love it."

"Wait," I say. "What if we did it this way?" Instead of falling to the floor, I wilt slowly, more gracefully, letting my arms float above me.

The other girls try the move, and it looks spooky. I wrap my arms around myself, and Nio smiles.

"I'm not sure what that has to do with fear either," Logan says.

"We could do both," Nio suggests.

Both Logan and I turn and glare at him. Then Logan says, "I have one other move from my improv I want to include." She does a running leap into a shoulder roll. "How about that?" she says.

Before I can stop myself, I say, "Are you going to add handsprings and aerials to the dance too?"

"Why not?" Logan says. "We've got ballet in it."

I feel like stamping my foot. Instead, I say, "I wanted to include a jump too." Then I run across the floor and leap into a switch split, one leg shooting forward and then back to create a scissor effect. I do another leap and then step into a handstand and complete Logan's shoulder roll. It hurts to do without a mat, and I worry I've tweaked my neck, but I don't care.

Logan frowns at me and then turns to Nio, all innocence. "I was just suggesting a fall. I'm not sure why she's getting all huffy."

"I'm not huffy," I say. "I'm just not sure that fall is right for our dance."

"Why don't you just try it?" Logan says.

"I will," I say. "When I get back from the bathroom." I turn and leave the studio. Once outside, I've got too much nervous energy to go hide in the bathroom. Instead, I circle the building. I could try the fall, but not in front of everyone. I stop. I don't have to do this. I could just not be in this stupid group. My shoulders relax at the thought. "I don't have to dance in that group," I say out loud, and I feel even better.

I wait outside the studio for Nio to come out. He stops when he sees me. "I wish you hadn't left. We made so much progress at the end of class. We're really working well together now."

"That's probably because I wasn't there," I say.

"No, that's not it at all."

We start walking to the dining hall. "Well, I think it is," I say. "In fact, I don't think I should be in the group."

Nio stops. "But we need you."

"You really don't. You've got Logan," I say, and then I walk away.

Fourteen

That evening, instead of eating in the dining hall, we have a cookout in the outer field of the camp. It's hotter in the straw-like grass away from the water and also more buggy. The heat makes the air appear to move in waves.

The counselors have set up four stations: softball, line dancing, archery and a dinner station of hotdogs and corn. I slap at mosquitoes and force myself to participate. I strike out in baseball and hide in the outfield when my team is at bat. I go through the motions of line dancing, even though it seems stupider than any other dance I've done. During archery I attempt to shoot arrows at the hay bale. I can't hit the target, but I'm no worse than anyone else.

As the sun starts to set, we all climb a small hill overlooking the lake and sit around a bonfire. One of the counselors plays guitar as the sun sets into the lake, turning the water pink and orange.

Just as I'm starting to relax, there's a tap on my shoulder. I turn, and there's Nio. "Can you come with me for a second?" he asks.

I follow him down the hill. "What's up?" I say.

Nio walks until we're out of sight of the other campers. Then he stops and turns to me. "We're having a dance rehearsal," he says. "Right now."

"But I'm not in your group anymore."

"Yeah, about that." Nio rubs his forehead. "Look, our dance sucks because of you and Logan fighting. And I chose you two because I think you're two of the best dancers and I wanted you to be in my group." He pauses for a minute and pushes his hair out of his eyes. "I wanted our dance to be about something real, something important. I know you've never danced your real fears in class. I haven't either, so I want to do it for you now."

"Here?"

He nods.

I rub my temples. "What if I don't want to see it?"

"I thought maybe if I danced mine, then you would dance yours."

"Yeah, I don't think so," I say.

Nio stretches his arms over his head and then lets them fall to his sides. "Meg, at school there are kids who want to beat the crap out of me every day because I dance. And I can't talk to anyone about it at home. But here I can. And I can dance it. I wanted to plan a dance around that fear, but I couldn't imagine talking about it in front of the entire class, so I thought we could choreograph it together. So please, do me a favor and watch my dance before I go home and have to pretend to have a girlfriend, okay?"

I suck in my lips. We stand looking at each other for a moment and then I say, "Okay."

Nio backs away from me and I sit down in the long, scratchy grass. The sound of campers singing "I've Been Working on the Railroad" wafts down the hill. Then Nio starts to move slowly, as if he can hear a song in his head. He starts to waltz in a circle in the grass, pretending to hold a partner the way he held me the other night. Heat climbs up my face as Nio moves his imaginary partner through different ballroom steps. The expression on his face is so soft, it's embarrassing to watch.

Then his dance becomes faster and more aggressive, and although he's still dancing with a pretend partner, he's also fighting that person. He looks confused. I want to look away, but I also want to keep watching. I sigh with relief when he stops dancing, when he whirls away from the confusion. He stands before me, sweating and panting. Then he stumbles away to swig from his water bottle and lies down, half-hidden in the grass.

For a moment neither of us says anything. I've never thought of dance being that personal.

Then Nio rolls over and looks at me. "Your turn," he says.

"I'm not like you. I don't have those kinds of fears," I whisper. I try to imagine Nio standing up in front of the contemporary dancers and describing his dance. I can see how hard that would be.

Nio drinks more water. "What about being scared of trying new things?"

I get up from the ground. "I can't believe you would say that. I've done nothing but try new things all week. And if I can do this camp, this class, then I have nothing to fear." My voice gets louder. "Everything else in my life is only hard work. And if I work hard, I can do it." *If only I really believed that.*

"What about being scared of that fall Logan wanted to put in the dance?"

I ignore him. "You want to see my dance? It's called *I Have No Fear.*" Then I back away from him, and with two small running steps I leap into a grand jeté. When I land, I step into an arabesque and then twist into a series of turns. Nio's frowning face spins by. I end with my arms lifted above my head, my head tipped back. Then I curtsy.

Nio doesn't clap. He crosses his arms against his chest, frowning. "What if you don't make it?"

"What?" My arms wilt at my sides. I can't help it.

"I said, what if you don't make it?"

"Have you been talking to Logan?" I can't help sneering as I say her name. I lift my arms and prepare for another turn, but Nio's "what if you don't make it" echoes in my head, and I wobble out of the turn, almost tumbling.

"I know you were scared to do the move Logan suggested this morning. And I think if you use that fear, you'll be an even more amazing dancer." Nio pauses. "Show me your real fear dance."

I stand, my arms again wilted at my sides. Nio's right. This is the emotion Mrs. G wants me to make an audience feel. And this is the time to show it—here, in this field, with only Nio watching.

Slowly I walk toward the space where Nio danced, where he trampled down the grass with his confused waltz. I tuck myself into a ball with my arms overhead and try to pretend Nio isn't here, try to think how to move. I remember Mom reading me Mrs. G's email, and I feel the fear that gripped my heart. I let that feeling spread throughout my body until my feet start to tap under me, slowly at first, and then faster and faster until I feel like the fear is going to explode out of me.

Then I step to the side, my arms spreading wide as if to throw the fear away. I tuck myself back into a ball, hiding my head again, my feet still tapping. I repeat the steps, warming up, and then I start the developpé. My left leg comes up high to the side; then I tip off-center. I don't bother with either of the fall moves Logan and I came up with. Instead, I contract my stomach muscles as if I've been punched in the gut, then crumple to the ground. *Yes*, I think. *This is how fear feels.*

And then something changes in me. I'm not just dancing steps through the high grass; I'm dancing the feeling in my head, in my heart. I start doing Logan's dance, the quick hand movements—then I interrupt it with the crumpling fall I just came up with, my arms reaching in front of me. I pick myself up and continue Logan's dance until I think about how it would feel not to be a ballerina. Again I drop to the ground as a surge of fear rushes through me. I don't have to pretend to show it on my face because it's already there.

My fear isn't going to go away—but maybe I can let it help me. Like Nio, I can use it to connect with my audience. I can make him feel my emotion, the way he did with me in his dance. I dance until I'm exhausted, until my knees feel bruised from falling. When I finally run out of energy, I collapse once more, slowly this time, and lie in the grass, listening to my heart race.

A moment passes. Nio calls "Meg?" from out in the shadows.

I lift one arm above the grass, and Nio crawls toward me. It's almost too dark to see each other, but Nio holds out one hand and pulls me up to sitting. "That was crazy," he says. "You have to do that for our group."

"Okay," I say, still breathing hard.

"And," Nio says, "you have to talk to Logan."

I hesitate. "She won't want to."

"Tell her you're doing it for me."

I nod my head. "Okay."

Fifteen

By the time Nio and I join the others, the campfire is winding down and the counselors are starting to gather their campers to walk back to the cabins. I want to talk to Logan right away, to get it over with, but also to show her the new fall move I've come up with while I'm still excited. I slip in and around campers, looking for her, and then I spot her walking through the field with some other girls from our cabin. "Hey," I say. "I've been looking for you."

"That's odd. Usually you avoid me." She keeps walking.

"Wait," I say. "I need to talk to you."

"What for?"

"It's about our group."

"I heard you're not even in it anymore."

"No, I am. I talked with Nio. Actually, I danced for him."

"Great." Logan licks her lips. "Just make up your mind. You're in, you're out."

"I'm in."

"That's too bad. We made a lot more progress after you left."

"Well, I'm in the group. I have to be. And I came up with this other fall move I want to do, and..." I hesitate. "I was wondering if you'll teach me your fall, the one into the push-up position."

She looks at me carefully. "Why would I do that?"

"Because I can do all the other moves except that one."

Logan stops walking and puts her hands on her hips. "So if I don't teach it to you, then you can't be in the group?"

I take a deep breath. "No. I could get Nio or one of the other girls to teach me."

"So don't bother me." Logan starts walking faster to catch up with the other girls. I jog to keep up with her.

"Look." I grab her arm. "I'm not here to steal Nio or take anything from you. I just came to learn some new things. And I've got this whole routine I made up from our moves, and it's all based on your idea, about falling, and I want to stop fighting with you, but I need your help. And I thought if I asked you to teach me the fall, then you wouldn't hate me so much."

Logan stops. We're on the edge of the field, near the cabins. The other girls are all ahead of us. The only light is from the dance hall ahead, the porch lights swarming with insects. "I don't hate you. I just think you're really annoying."

I throw my hands up in the air. "Well, that's too bad, but if you want our dance to be good, you'll have to put up with me."

"Yeah, forget it." She turns to walk away, but I grab her arm.

"Look, this is Nio's dance, the dance that expresses all the things...all the things he can't say at home. Are you going to be the one who ruins it for him?"

Logan's scrunched-up brow and clenched teeth release. "Fine, I'll do it for Nio, but don't think I'm doing it just to help you." She steps away from me to show me the move. "You just lift your arms on one side and bring them over your head, and then you fall slowly and catch yourself." She demonstrates, making it look easy.

I step away to try it. My arms come over my head and I start falling, but I can't let go. I jut my leg forward at the last minute, breaking the line of my body. I try again, gritting my teeth, but I can't do it. I expect Logan to sneer, but she looks sympathetic. "It would be easier in water," she says. "You could try it tomorrow afternoon."

"No, there would be too many people watching. And I want to learn it now so we can get on with our choreography."

"You mean your choreography." She does a feeble imitation of the developpé step.

"Look, you're right. The dance should be about falling. I came up with this other fall move I think we should put in. It goes like this." Before she has a chance to walk away, I do the new fall.

Logan watches, eyes squinted critically. "It's not bad."

"You see, it starts with one fall, the graceful one I showed you, and then it builds to this fall, and then finally to the one I can't do yet."

"Girls, you're supposed to be in the cabin," Tara calls.

"In a second," Logan calls back.

"Watch," I say. And I perform her hand movements from earlier, combining them first with the graceful fall, then with the one I came up with tonight and then with the windmill one, except that I can't do it.

"You just have to let go. Give in to that fear," Logan says. "What's the worst thing that will happen?"

I think about the dream I had about the move. "I'll smash my face?"

"No." She laughs. "You might hurt your wrist. That's all."

"I don't want that to happen either."

Logan does the fall again, and then she says, "Wait. Try it this way." She steps into arabesque and then puts her hands to the ground, one leg coming up high in the back before coming down to the push-up. "How about this?"

I take a breath and step into the arabesque. Then I tilt over until my hands are on the ground and slowly come down into a push-up. "I can do that." I repeat the move, and then Logan does it with me.

"Girls, you need to come in now," Tara calls.

Logan and I both freeze. "Don't say anything," she whispers, and we step back, away from the light. "Do it again."

We practice the move again and again, doing it faster, until it's less of an arabesque and more of a fall, until we're doing it at the same time, the two of us falling in the shadows together.

Sixteen

Once Logan and I stop fighting, the rest of the choreography comes together easily. We start our dance in pairs, moving to Nio's waltz. Slowly it becomes more of a battle, and then it changes into the fight dance the younger girls composed. As the intensity of the drums builds, we move into Logan's dance with its anxious hand movements, combined with the falls we came up with together, and the battement developpé. The windmill fall becomes so easy for me that I can do it as well as any ballet move. We also include some of the leaps and jumps we all wanted. Logan and I aren't exactly friends, but she treats me the same as everyone else, which is a relief.

All I can think about is our dance. I run through the steps in my head all day. I love the dance not only because of its intensity, but also because it's filled with my own ideas.

* * *

One day during lunch, the director announces that anyone interested in costuming should come to an orientation session that afternoon. Next to me, Logan's arm shoots into the air. Then, on my other side, Jodie grabs my arm and lifts it high.

"What are you doing?" I ask.

"You want to do costuming," Jodie says.

"I do?"

"You do."

"Why?"

"You have style, remember?"

"Oh, right."

I look over at Logan to see what she thinks about me doing costuming too, but she's too excited to care. "I have an amazing idea for our dance," I hear her telling Cassidy.

Still, I'm a little nervous when I show up at the costuming room and Logan sees me. She stiffens for a moment and looks away, but I'm distracted by the racks and racks of fluffy skirts, sequined tops, fringed capes and shiny leotards. I let out a long sigh. Right away I start designing a costume. I choose a pale pink leotard and soft tulle skirt with sequins around the waist and a black feather boa. "Say you were dancing a really sad pas de deux," I say to Logan. "This is what you should wear."

Logan pulls a red dress and black shawl off another rack. "Or maybe this."

I smile and hand her a small black hat with a veil. "A hat would add a more modern look."

"Ooh, I like that."

I shrug. "Thanks." Then I start looking through a rack of hot pants.

"I am going to do costuming for my school's theater department next year," Logan says.

"What do you mean?" I ask, relieved that Logan is talking to me so casually.

"You get to choose the costumes for the school play. My high school has a good theater program, and my drama teacher says you can even get a job doing it. Imagine, you could have your own designs onstage for everyone to see."

"Huh, I never thought of that." I imagine choosing costumes for a ballet. I'd love to do a really different take on *Swan Lake* or *Giselle*, something beautiful but not traditional. I wander over to the desk and start sketching on scrap paper.

"Whatcha doing?" Logan asks.

"I'm planning ballet costumes." I look up and grin. "I'll send them to you after we go home."

Logan nods. "Cool."

* * *

On the day of the final performance, we all go back to our cabins after lunch to get ready for the dress rehearsal. The ballroom dancers struggle into their gowns and clack through the cabin in their high heels. Jodie and Cassidy wear overalls and straw hats for a musical comedy number. I pull on the one-piece metallic-blue bodysuit Logan chose for our group. The suit covers my body from my ankles to my wrists and even has a hood that covers my hair, but I feel naked in it. A puddle of sweat blooms along my spine as soon as I pull it on. For a moment I miss the pretty tutus of ballet, but I know the shiny costumes will look incredible onstage.

At one o'clock Tara starts shooing everyone to the main hall. Despite cries for more time to finish hair and makeup, no one needs much urging.

If I thought the hall was loud on the first day, today the noise is earsplitting. The energy level is so high, I feel like I might explode. We all sit in our groups, our costumes and makeup already on, except for the ballroom dancers, who are first to perform. Tonight, when the hall is full of parents and friends, there won't be any room for us to watch, so this dress rehearsal is our chance to see the other dances. I sit with Logan and Nio and the others and look at the program. It's already limp from my sweaty palms. Our dance is listed as *Falling*, a name Nio suggested. I try to imagine the program in my drawer at home with the rest of my dance keepsakes. Earlier in the week I never would have wanted to keep it, but now I'm looking forward to showing it to Julia so she can see what I helped create.

When the lights dim, a huge cheer rises from the campers, and goose bumps form on my arms. Tara takes the stage, and we cheer. She smiles and holds up her hand for quiet. "Welcome to the fifteenth annual Camp Dance Extravaganza!"

We clap and cheer and catcall so loudly, she can't go on. When we finally settle down, she says, "I promise this will be a performance you will never forget, not only because of the tappers, ballroom, contemporary, hip-hop and jazz dancers, but because YOU were part of the show."

I shiver as dancers scream and clap around me. I'm smiling so hard my jaw aches.

Tara goes on. "All week you have choreographed, rehearsed, revised and created amazing works of art. Dancers, you should be so proud of all your hard work. Each and every one of you is incredibly talented." We cheer again. "We have a very special lineup tonight. To start, we have the Salsa Mixers!"

Latin music fills the air, and girls burst onstage in red fringed dresses. After the ballroom dancers, the musical-theater group performs an ensemble piece from *Oklahoma*. Then the tappers dance, and it's time for the contemporary dancers to go backstage.

I join Nio and Logan and the others warming up. We're so excited that I'm not sure how we'll manage to look fearful. Already Olivia's group is onstage, and Logan and the other girls are bopping around to their song.

Nio beckons for us all to come together. He wraps his arms around us, and we stand in a tight huddle in the wings. "I want to thank you guys so much for working with me. I think I've wanted to do this ever since I realized most boys don't dance. Thank you for being the kind of people who were willing to expose your own fears for the sake of our group." Nio looks like he might cry, and I know if he does, I will too. He clears his throat and composes himself. "I know we're all really excited, but let's take a few minutes to get into the right head space."

We all nod and wander quietly away. I stretch my arms over my head and look down at the sweat marks already showing on the costume. I feel a flutter of excitement like I do before any performance, but this time it's even more special: this is *my* dance. When I do the moves, I feel them. And I know the audience will too.

Olivia's group comes offstage and the lights dim. As I move onto the stage, I fix a look of fear on my face, but inside I feel certain, my body powerful.

Like I can do anything.

Acknowledgments

I am thankful to my editor, Robin Stevenson, for her patience and guidance during the editing process. Also thanks to Catherine Allen and Amara Salloum for help correcting my dance terms. Lastly, I'm grateful to Rachel Speller for coming up with a title for this book.

LEANNE LIEBERMAN is the author of three YA novels: *Gravity, The Book of Trees* and *Lauren Yanofsky Hates the Holocaust.* Her fiction has been published in *Descant, The New Quarterly, Fireweed, The Antigonish Review* and other journals. These days Leanne only dances in her kitchen, but she still dreams from time to time that she's dancing onstage. Leanne lives in Kingston, Ontario.